For Hope Charlotte and family.
Grateful you popped up! —*A. D.*

For Jovita —*C. S.*

DANDY

Written by **Ame Dyckman** ❀ Illustrated by **Charles Santoso**

L **B**

LITTLE, BROWN AND COMPANY
NEW YORK   BOSTON

Daddy spied something scary
on his perfect lawn.

He ran for his clippers. . . .

But he was too late.

"Hi, Daddy!"

"Sweetie!" Daddy said. "That's a weed!"

"A flower," Sweetie said. "Her name is Charlotte. She's my best friend."

Daddy hoped his friends wouldn't notice.

He tried during book time.

But Sweetie was there.

"Hi, Daddy!"

He tried during nap time.

He tried during snack time.

But Sweetie was there.

"Hi, Daddy!
We saved you a spot!"

Once again, Daddy hoped his friends wouldn't notice.

Daddy got serious.

But Sweetie was ALWAYS there.

"Hi, Daddy!"

Until it was time for swim lessons.

"Bye, Daddy!
Take care of Charlotte!"

"I will!" Daddy said.

He couldn't wait.

But Daddy spied something else on his
once perfect lawn: Sweetie's painting.

"I can't do it," Daddy cried.

WE KNOW!

(They were daddies, too.)

Then Daddy's snips . . . slipped.

They knew what they had to do.

Everyone hoped Sweetie wouldn't notice.

She did.

"Daddy!" Sweetie cried.
"There's something WRONG with Charlotte!"

"LOOK!"

Daddy looked at his lawn.

He looked at his little girl.

He chose.

"It'll be okay, Sweetie," Daddy said. "Watch."

And soon . . .

"Hi, Daddy!" Sweetie said.
"Meet Charlotte Two! And Charlotte Three!
And Charlotte Four! And . . ."

Sweetie beamed. "Aren't they beautiful?"

Daddy smiled. "Yes, Sweetie," he said.
"They're ... DANDY."

AUTHOR'S NOTE

In our old neighborhood, the daddies took their lawn care VERY seriously.

When a dandelion popped up . . . WAR! WAR ON THE DANDELION!

We watched this instead of TV.

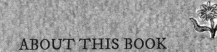

ABOUT THIS BOOK

The illustrations for this book were done digitally with handmade pencil textures on top. This book was edited by Mary-Kate Gaudet and designed by Jen Keenan. The production was supervised by Virginia Lawther, and the production editor was Marisa Finkelstein. The text was set in IM FELL DW Pica PRO, and the display type is hand-lettered by Jen Keenan.

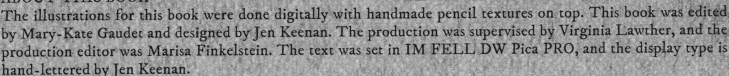